PLEASE WASH YOUR HANDS BEFORE YOU READ ME AND KEEP ME CLEAN

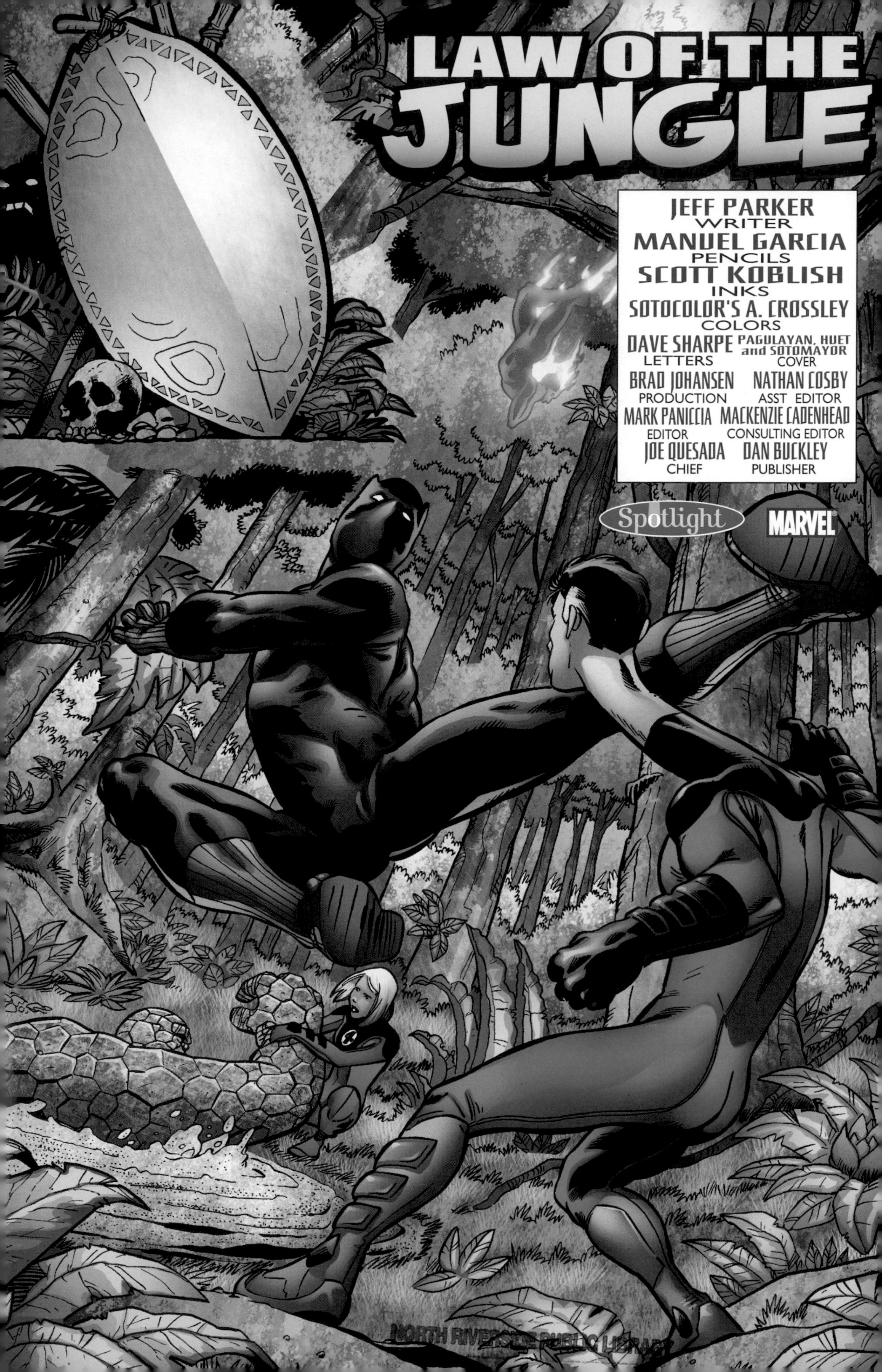
LAW OF THE JUNGLE
JEFF PARKER WRITER
MANUEL GARCIA PENCILS
SCOTT KOBLISH INKS
SOTOCOLOR'S A. CROSSLEY COLORS
DAVE SHARPE LETTERS
PAGULAYAN, HUET and SOTOMAYOR COVER
BRAD JOHANSEN PRODUCTION
NATHAN COSBY ASST EDITOR
MARK PANICCIA EDITOR
MACKENZIE CADENHEAD CONSULTING EDITOR
JOE QUESADA CHIEF
DAN BUCKLEY PUBLISHER
Spotlight
MARVEL

VISIT US AT
www.abdopublishing.com

Reinforced library bound edition published in 2008 by Spotlight, a division of the ABDO Publishing Group, 8000 West 78th Street, Edina, Minnesota 55439. Spotlight produces high-quality reinforced library bound editions for schools and libraries. Published by agreement with Marvel Characters, Inc.

Library of Congress Cataloging-in-Publication Data

Parker, Jeff, 1966-
  Law of the jungle / Jeff Parker, writer ; Manuel Garcia, pencils ; Scott Koblish, inks ; A. Crossley, colors ; Dave Sharpe, letters ; Pagulayan, Huet and Sotomayor, cover. -- Reinforced library bound ed.
      p. cm. -- (Fantastic Four)
  "Marvel age"--Cover.
  Revision of issue 10 of Marvel adventures Fantastic Four.
  ISBN 978-1-59961-390-1
  1. Graphic novels. I. Garcia, Manuel. II. Marvel adventures Fantastic Four. 10. III. Title.

PN6728.F33P36 2008
741.5'973--dc22

                                                              2007020255

All Spotlight books have reinforced library bindings and are manufactured in the United States of America.

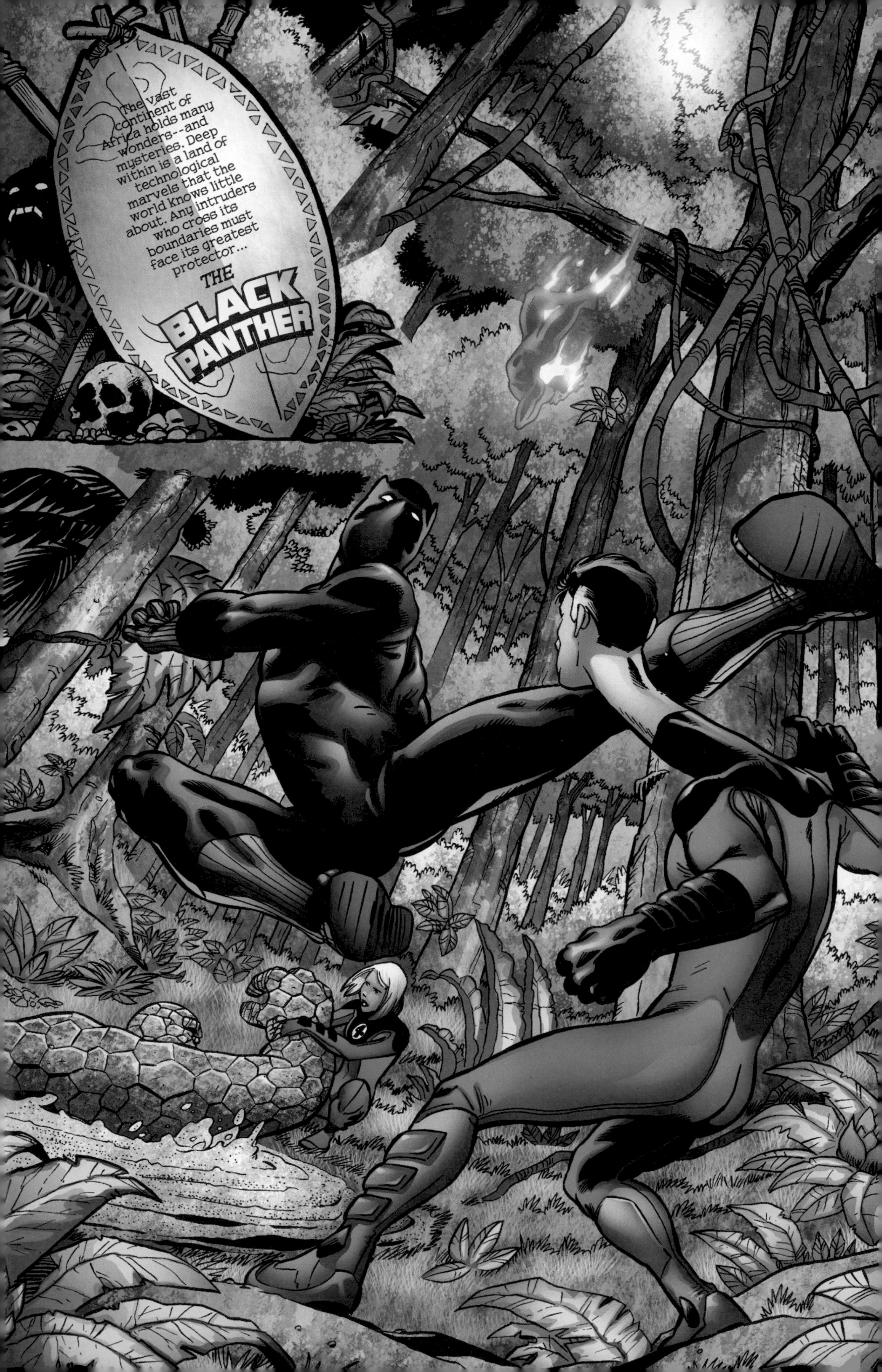
The vast continent of Africa holds many wonders--and mysteries. Deep within is a land of technological marvels that the world knows little about. Any intruders who cross its boundaries must face its greatest protector...
THE BLACK PANTHER

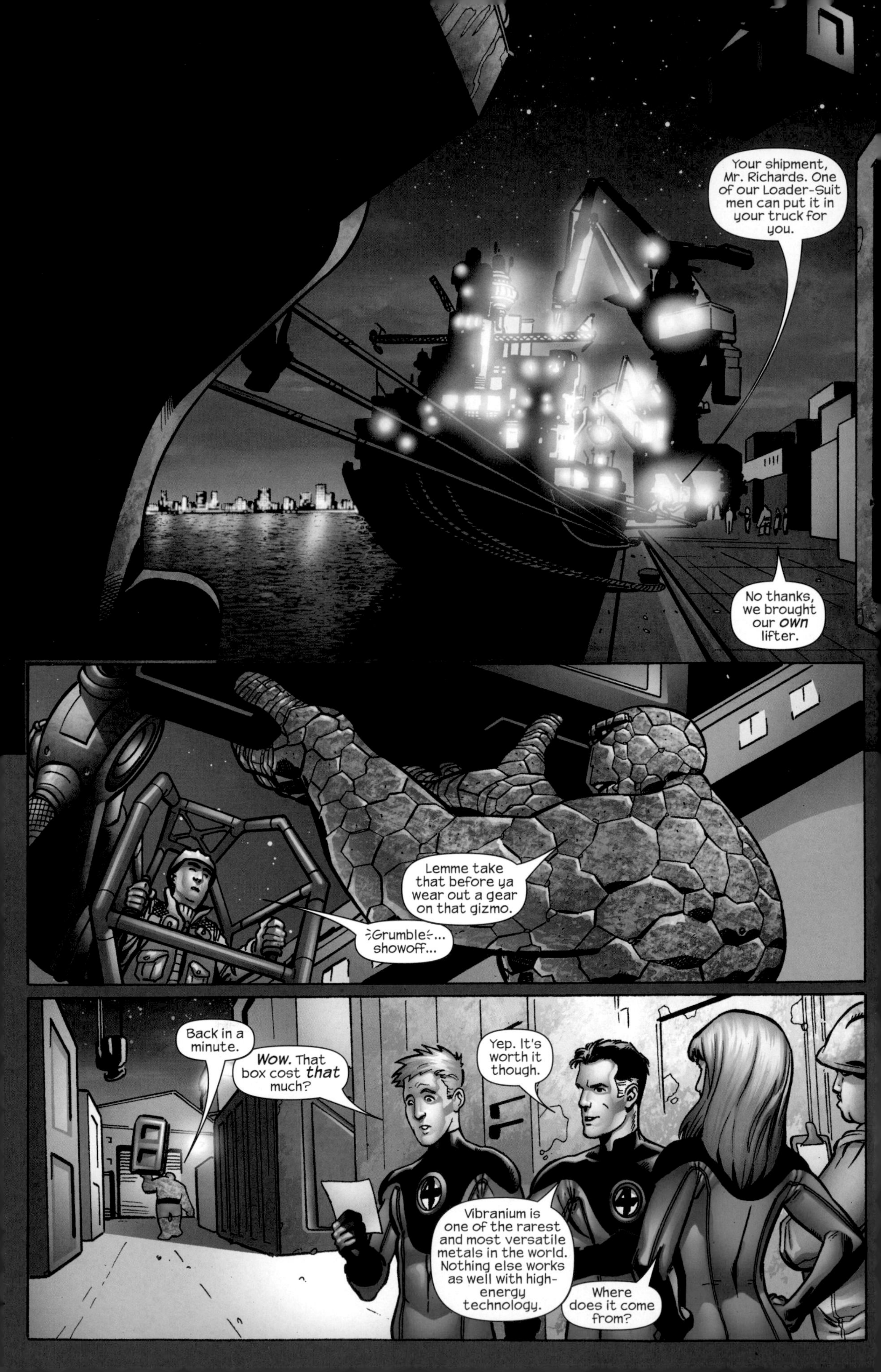
Your shipment, Mr. Richards. One of our Loader-Suit men can put it in your truck for you.
No thanks, we brought our OWN lifter.
Lemme take that before ya wear out a gear on that gizmo.
Grumble... showoff...
Back in a minute.
WOW. That box cost that much?
Yep. It's worth it though.
Vibranium is one of the rarest and most versatile metals in the world. Nothing else works as well with high-energy technology.
Where does it come from?

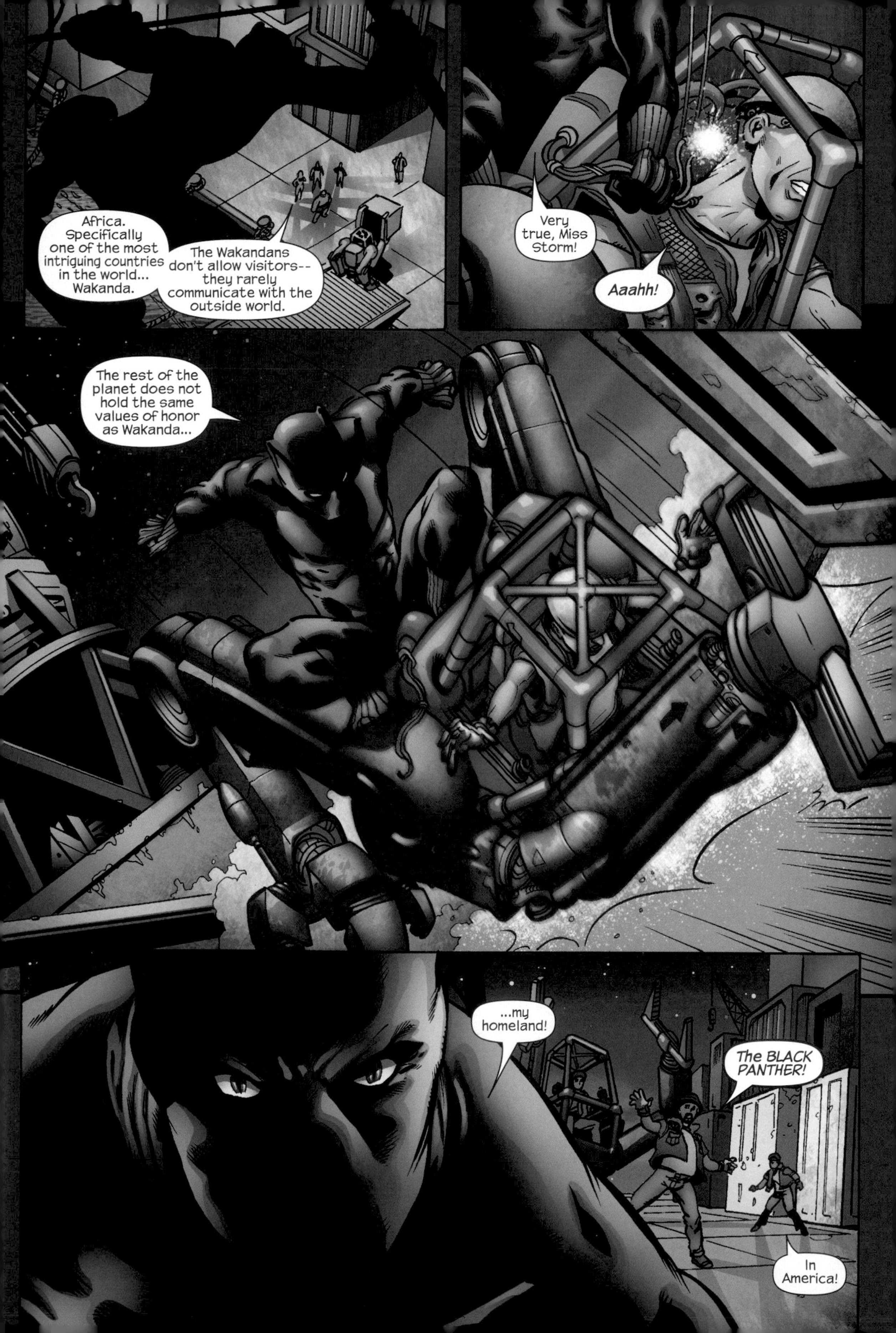

Africa. Specifically one of the most intriguing countries in the world... Wakanda.
The Wakandans don't allow visitors-- they rarely communicate with the outside world.
Very true, Miss Storm!
Aaahh!
The rest of the planet does not hold the same values of honor as Wakanda...
...my homeland!
The BLACK PANTHER!
In America!

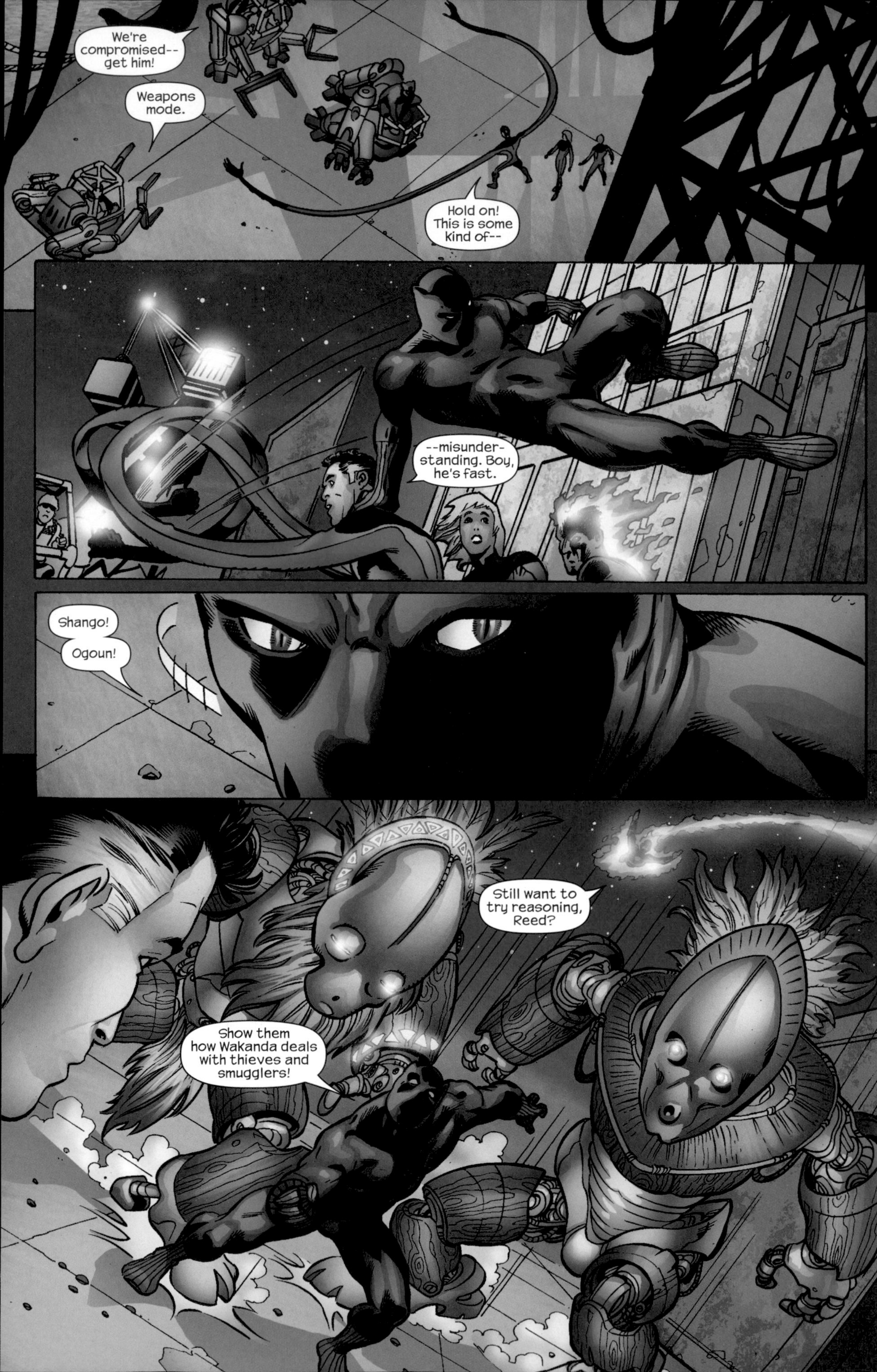
We're compromised--get him!
Weapons mode.
Hold on! This is some kind of--
--misunder-standing. Boy, he's fast.
Shango!
Ogoun!
Still want to try reasoning, Reed?
Show them how Wakanda deals with thieves and smugglers!

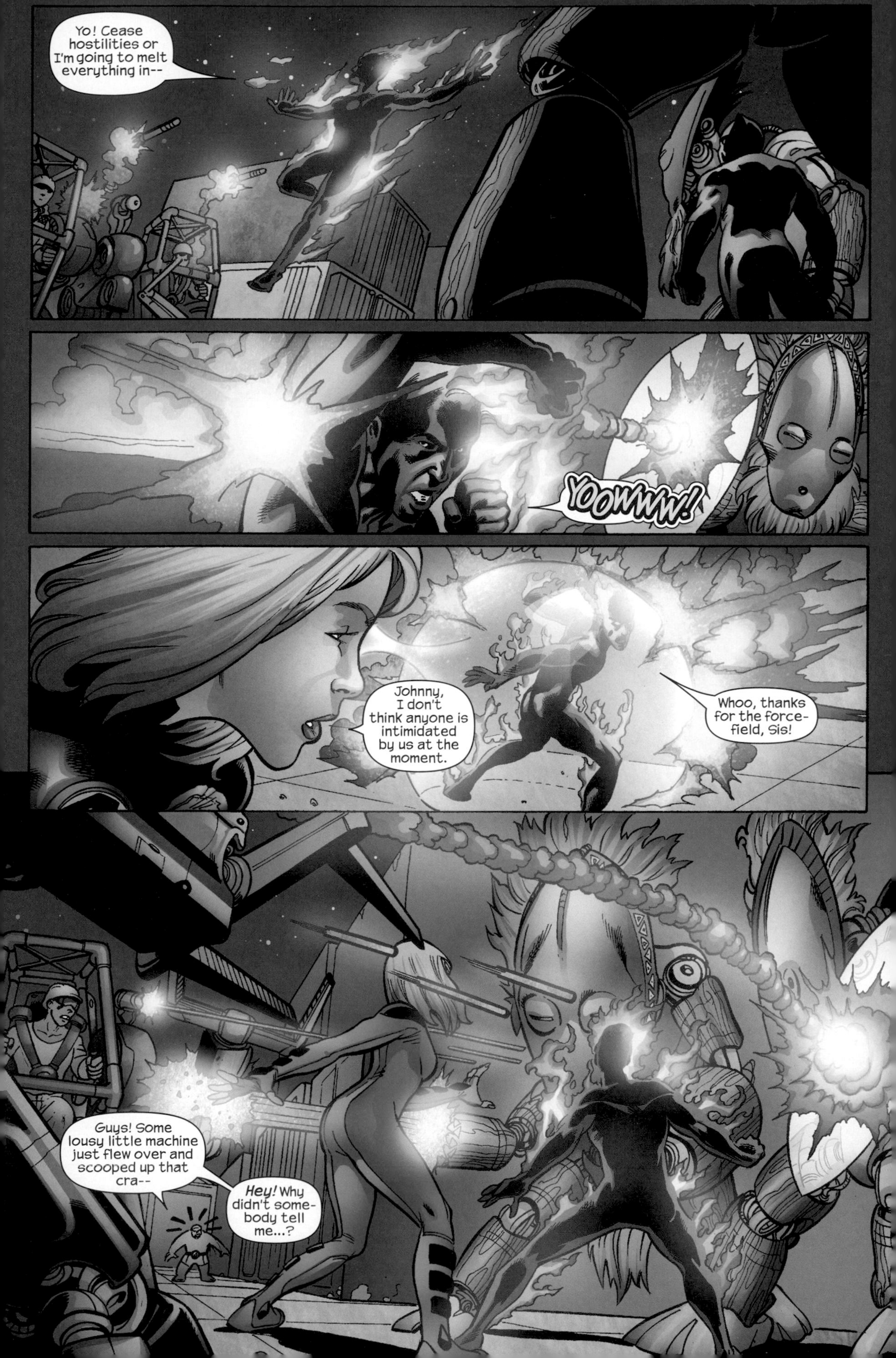
Yo! Cease hostilities or I'm going to melt everything in--
YOOWWW!
Johnny, I don't think anyone is intimidated by us at the moment.
Whoo, thanks for the force-field, Sis!
Guys! Some lousy little machine just flew over and scooped up that cra--
Hey! Why didn't some-body tell me...?

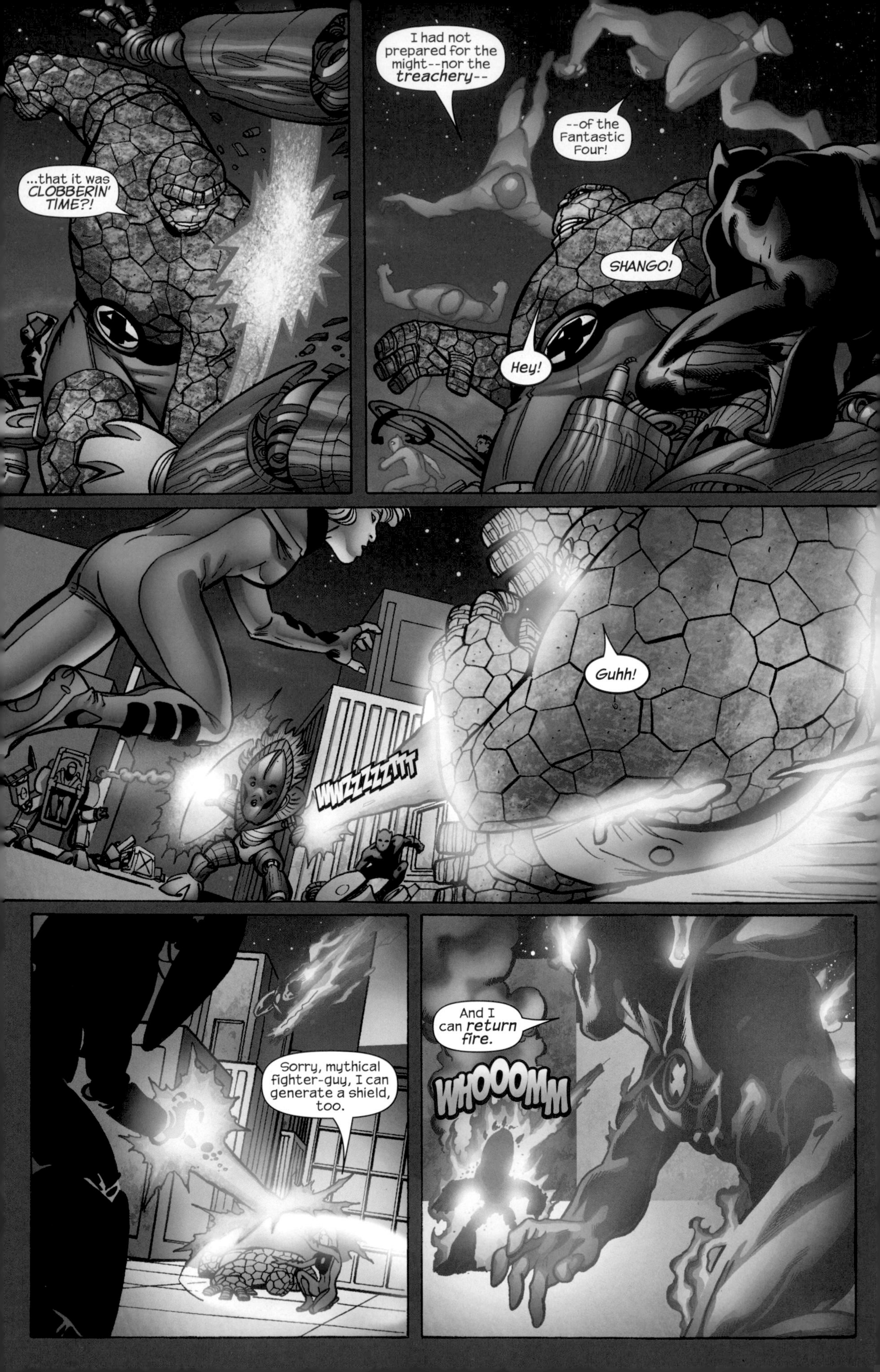

...that it was CLOBBERIN' TIME?!
I had not prepared for the might--nor the treachery--
--of the Fantastic Four!
SHANGO!
Hey!
Guhh!
WWZZZZZZTTT
Sorry, mythical fighter-guy, I can generate a shield, too.
And I can return fire.
WHOOOMM

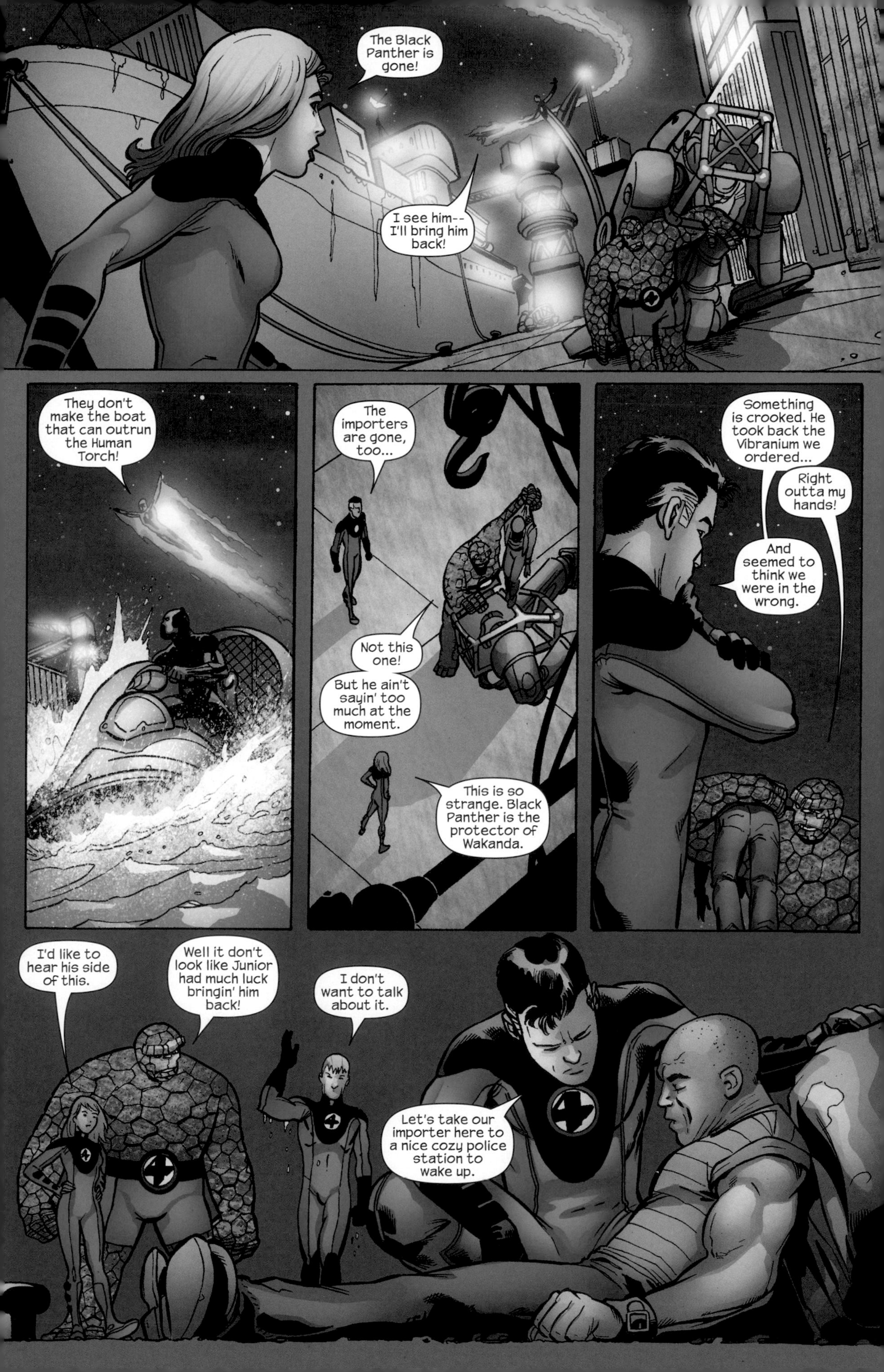
The Black Panther is gone!
I see him-- I'll bring him back!
They don't make the boat that can outrun the Human Torch!
The importers are gone, too...
Not this one!
But he ain't sayin' too much at the moment.
This is so strange. Black Panther is the protector of Wakanda.
Something is crooked. He took back the Vibranium we ordered...
Right outta my hands!
And seemed to think we were in the wrong.
I'd like to hear his side of this.
Well it don't look like Junior had much luck bringin' him back!
I don't want to talk about it.
Let's take our importer here to a nice cozy police station to wake up.

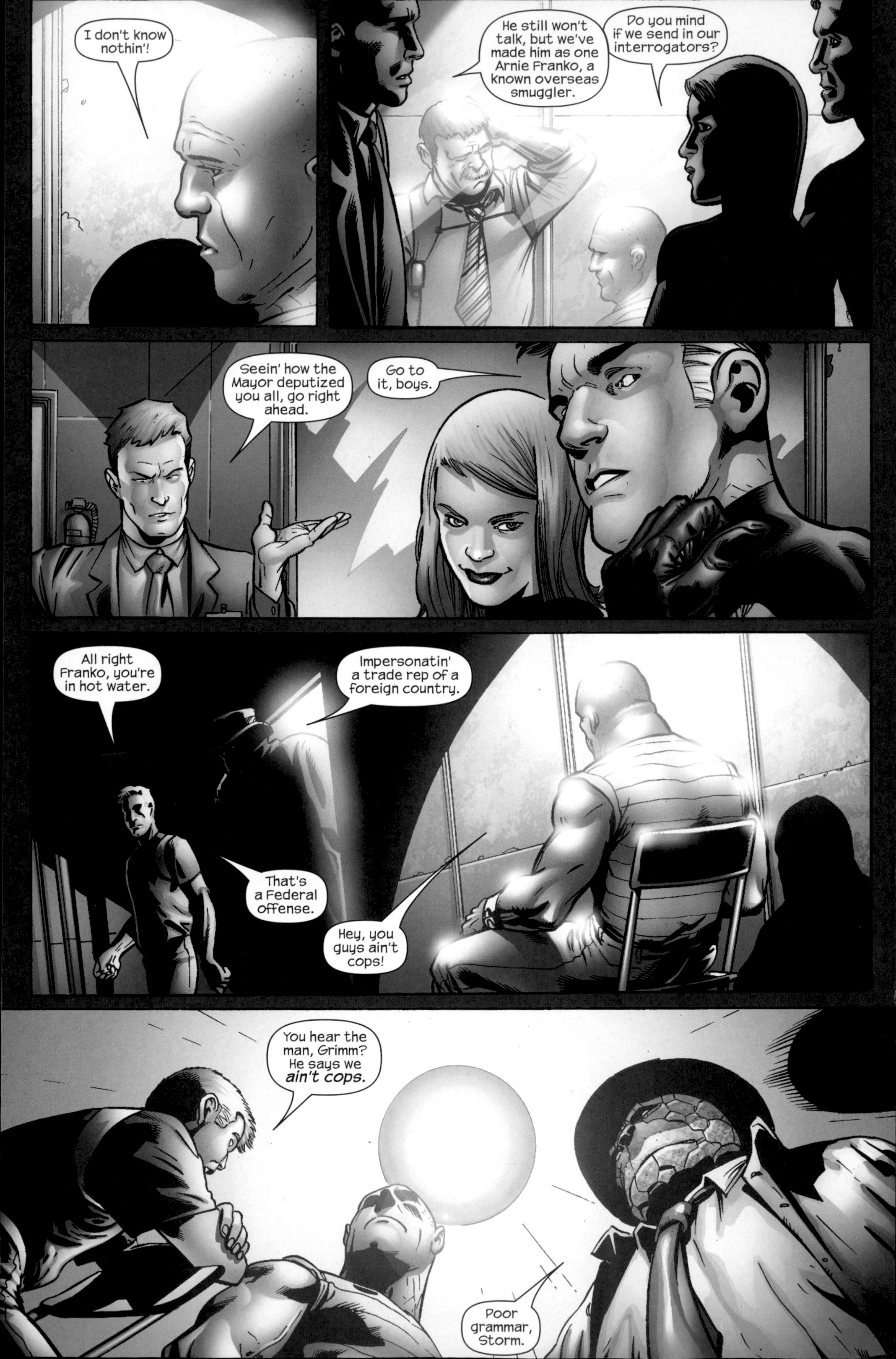
I don't know nothin'!
He still won't talk, but we've made him as one Arnie Franko, a known overseas smuggler.
Do you mind if we send in our interrogators?
Seein' how the Mayor deputized you all, go right ahead.
Go to it, boys.
All right Franko, you're in hot water.
Impersonatin' a trade rep of a foreign country.
That's a Federal offense.
Hey, you guys ain't cops!
You hear the man, Grimm? He says we *ain't cops.*
Poor grammar, Storm.

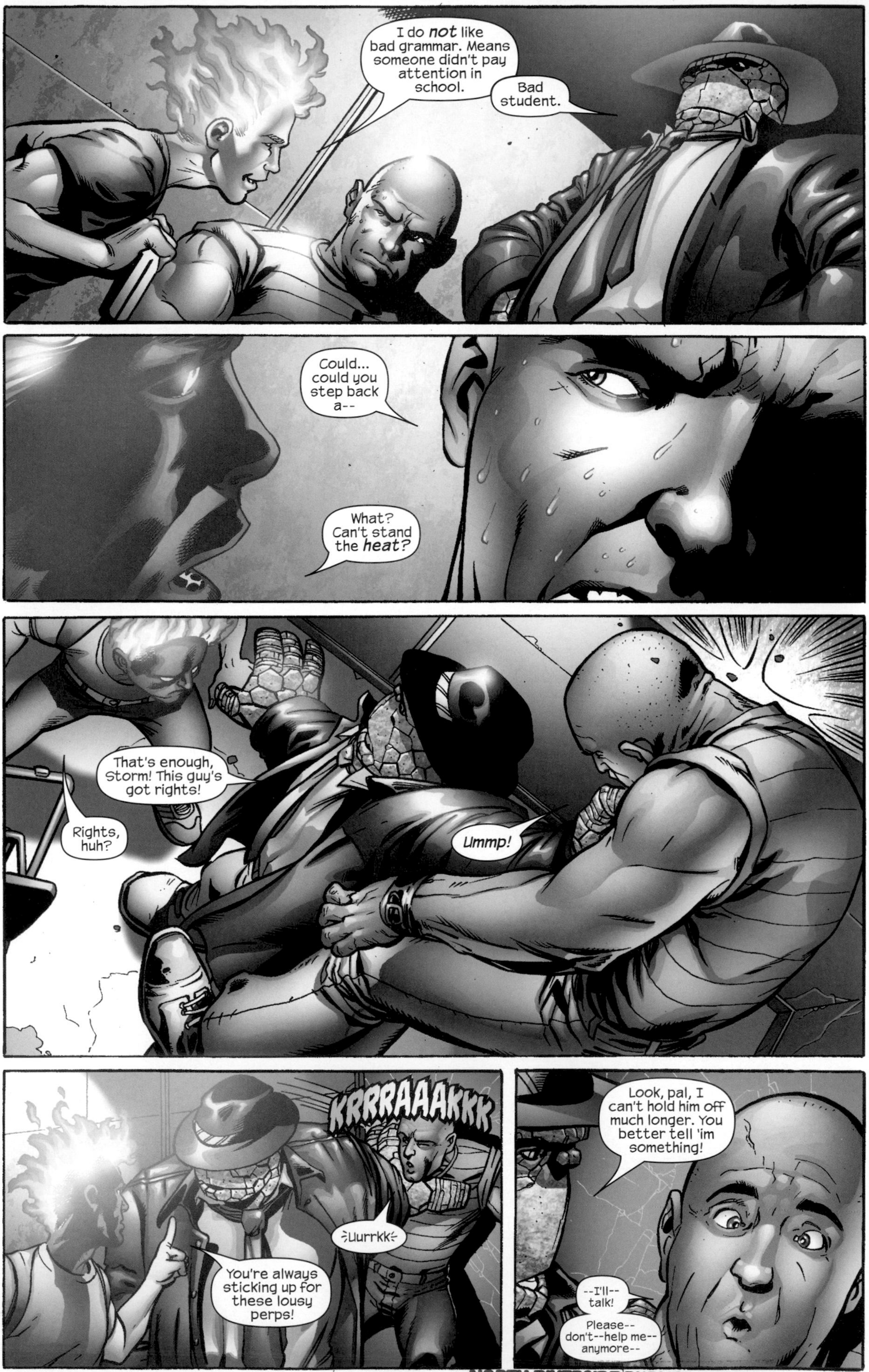
I do *not* like bad grammar. Means someone didn't pay attention in school.
Bad student.
Could... could you step back a--
What? Can't stand the *heat*?
That's enough, Storm! This guy's got rights!
Rights, huh?
Ummp!
KRRRAAAKKK
You're always sticking up for these lousy perps!
Uurrkk
Look, pal, I can't hold him off much longer. You better tell 'im something!
--I'll-- talk!
Please-- don't--help me-- anymore--

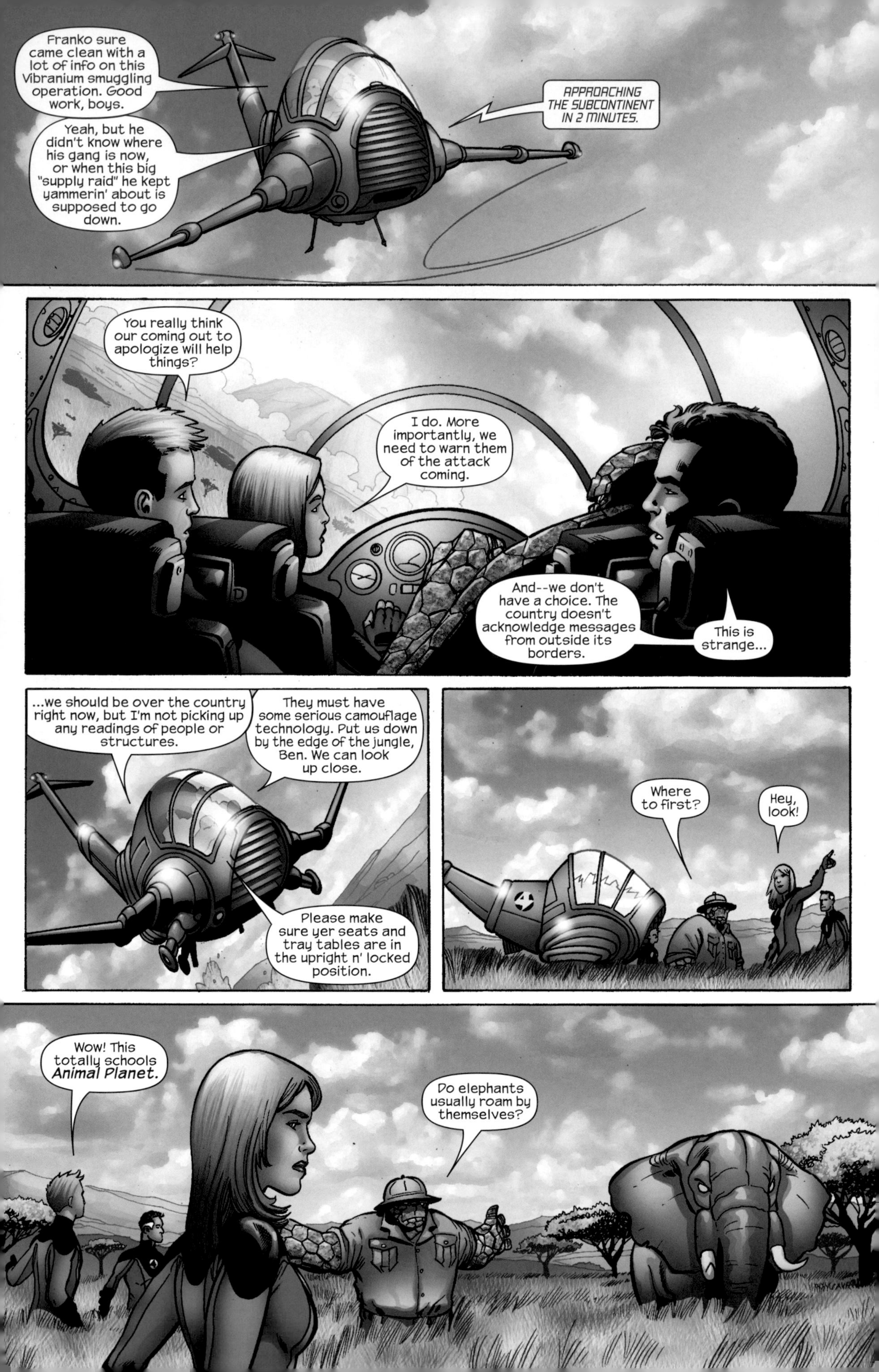
Franko sure came clean with a lot of info on this Vibranium smuggling operation. Good work, boys.
Yeah, but he didn't know where his gang is now, or when this big "supply raid" he kept yammerin' about is supposed to go down.
APPROACHING THE SUBCONTINENT IN 2 MINUTES.
You really think our coming out to apologize will help things?
I do. More importantly, we need to warn them of the attack coming.
And--we don't have a choice. The country doesn't acknowledge messages from outside its borders.
This is strange...
...we should be over the country right now, but I'm not picking up any readings of people or structures.
They must have some serious camouflage technology. Put us down by the edge of the jungle, Ben. We can look up close.
Please make sure yer seats and tray tables are in the upright n' locked position.
Where to first?
Hey, look!
Wow! This totally schools *Animal Planet.*
Do elephants usually roam by themselves?

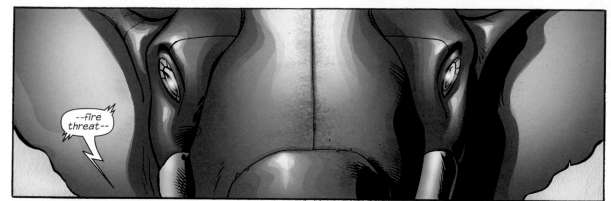

--fire threat--

--coat with non-combustible gel--

Ahgh! I'm always getting gooed!

Hey, that's no--

--elephant-- *whoa!* All right, buster, you're askin' for it!

Arrrhhh!

ZzzAAPZzzAAP

Whew!

Let him go, Ele-bot!

Every-one, into the jungle!

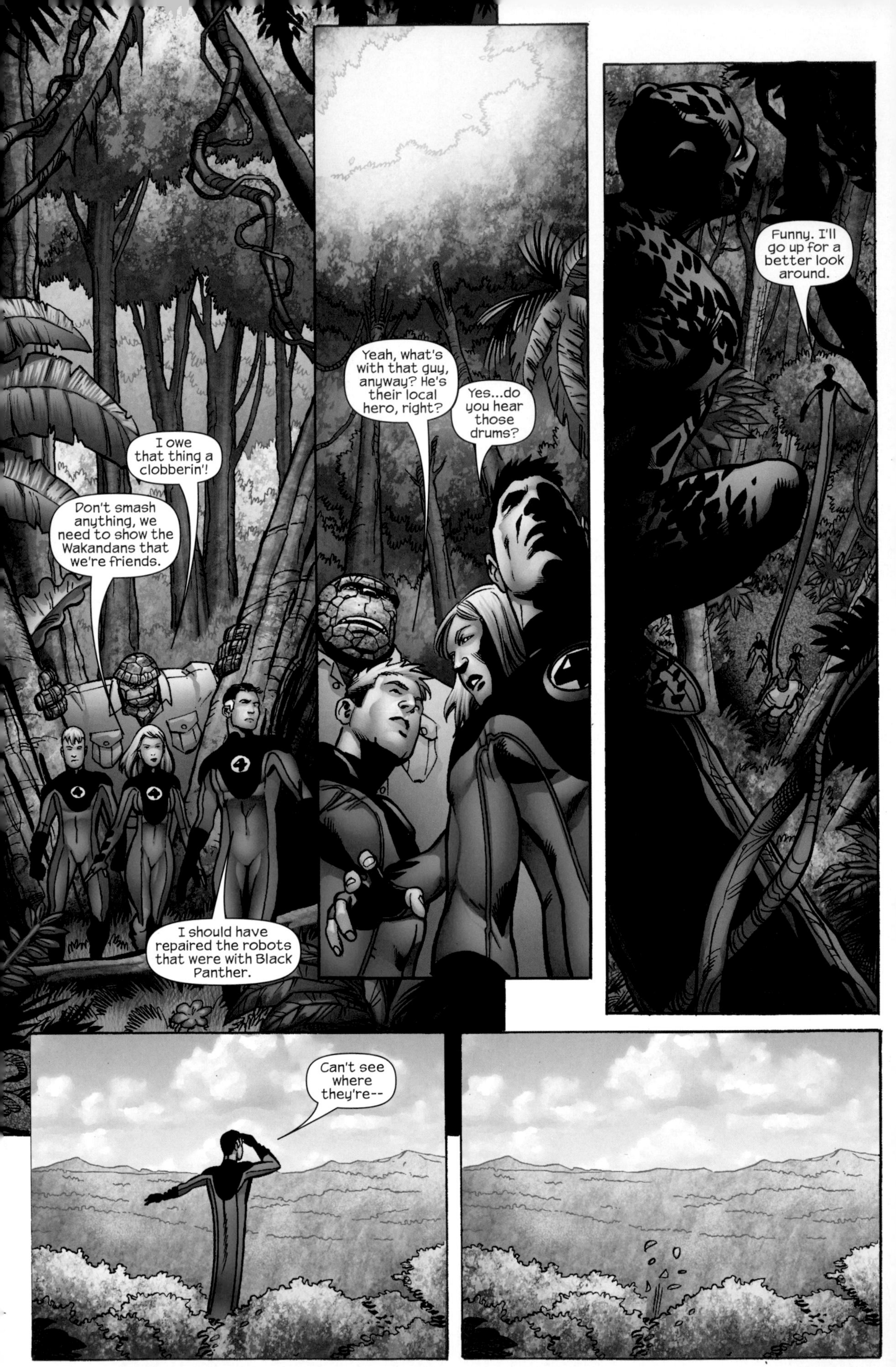
Don't smash anything, we need to show the Wakandans that we're friends.
I owe that thing a clobberin'!
I should have repaired the robots that were with Black Panther.
Yeah, what's with that guy, anyway? He's their local hero, right?
Yes...do you hear those drums?
Funny. I'll go up for a better look around.
Can't see where they're--

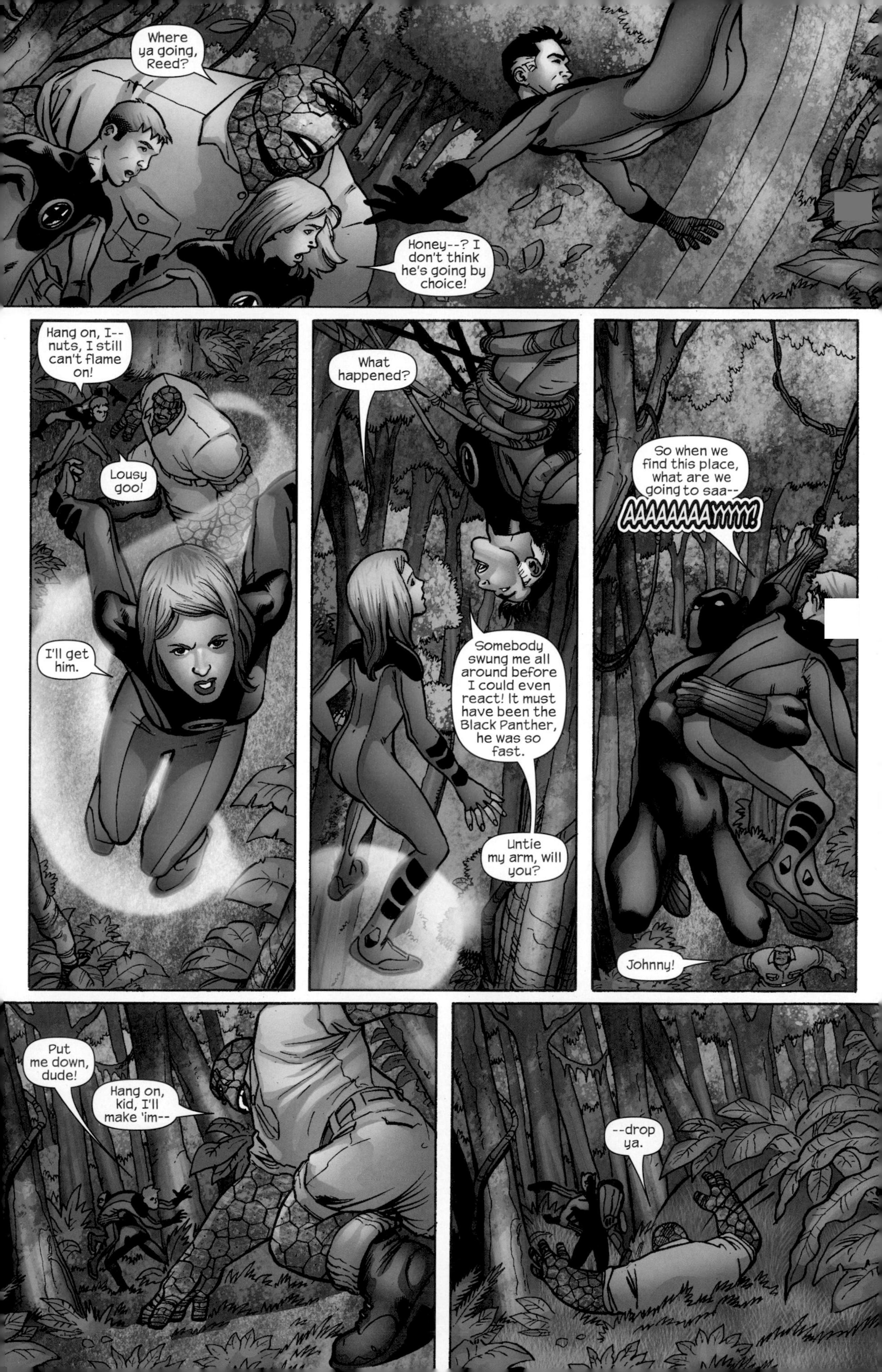
Where ya going, Reed?
Honey--? I don't think he's going by choice!
Hang on, I-- nuts, I still can't flame on!
Lousy goo!
I'll get him.
What happened?
Somebody swung me all around before I could even react! It must have been the Black Panther, he was so fast.
Untie my arm, will you?
So when we find this place, what are we going to saa--
AAAAAAAAYYYYY!
Johnny!
Put me down, dude!
Hang on, kid, I'll make 'im--
--drop ya.

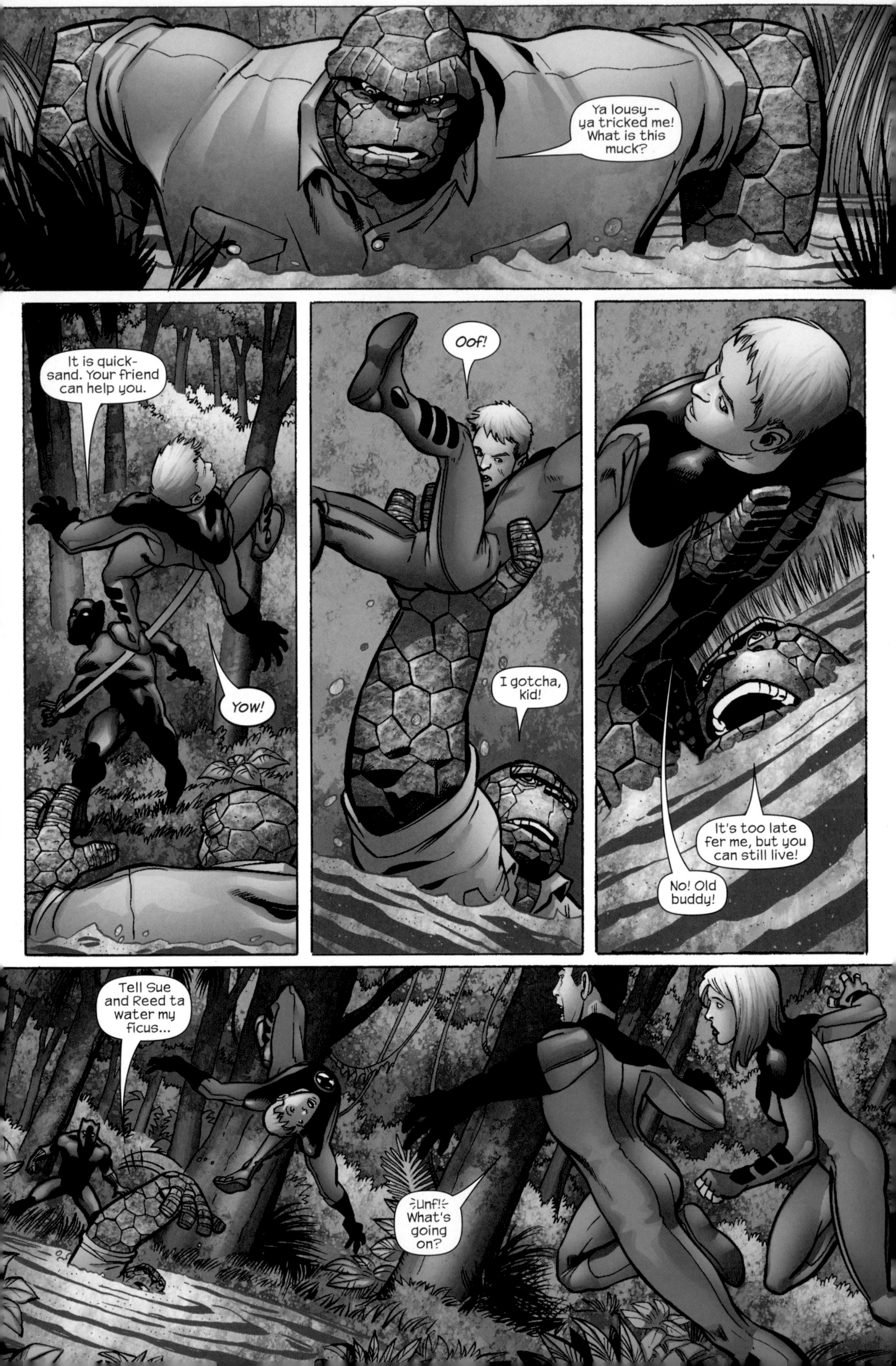
Ya lousy--
ya tricked me! What is this muck?
It is quick-sand. Your friend can help you.
YOW!
Oof!
I gotcha, kid!
It's too late fer me, but you can still live!
No! Old buddy!
Tell Sue and Reed ta water my ficus...
Unf! What's going on?

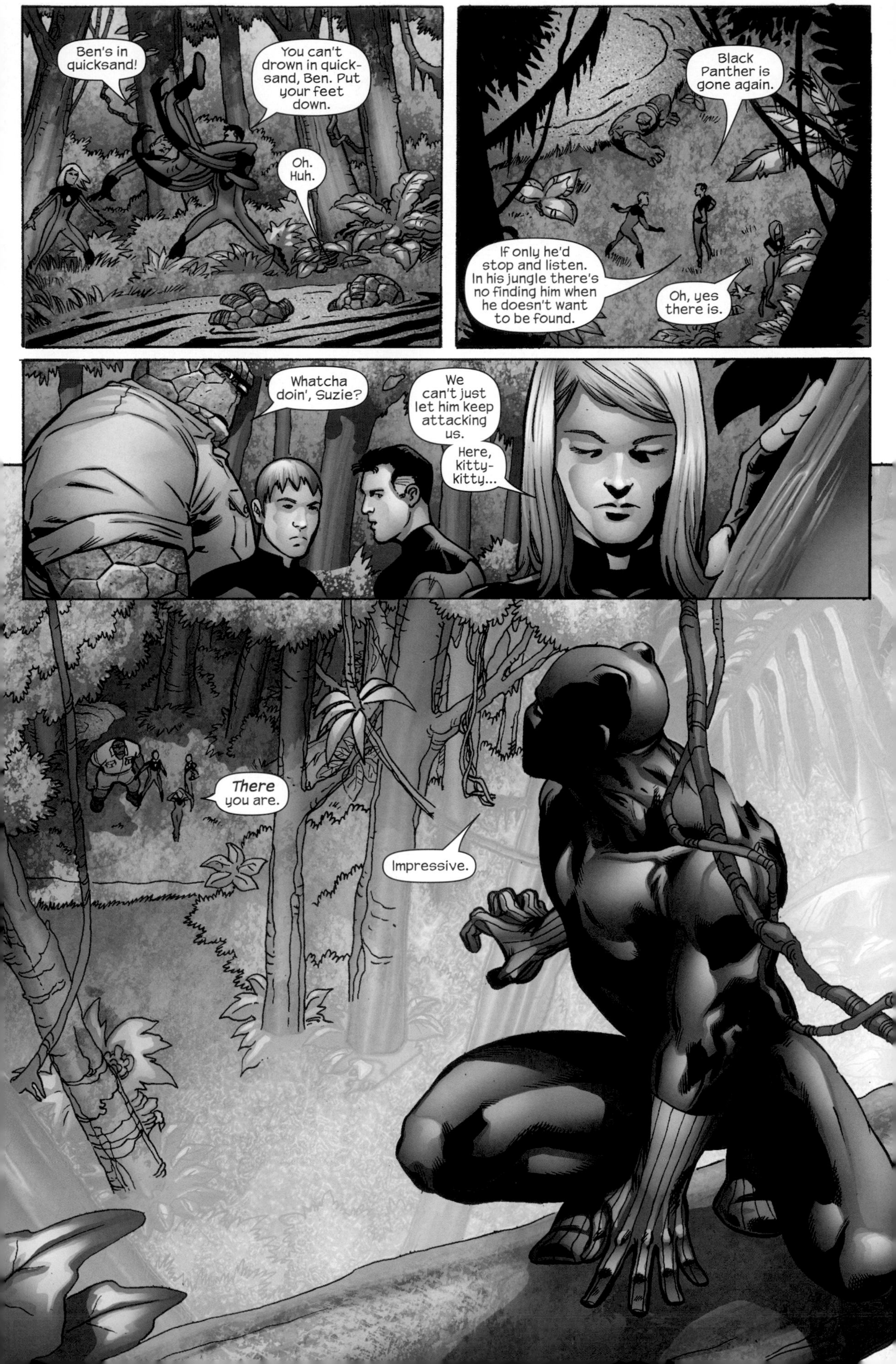
Ben's in quicksand!
You can't drown in quick-sand, Ben. Put your feet down.
Oh. Huh.
Black Panther is gone again.
If only he'd stop and listen. In his jungle there's no finding him when he doesn't want to be found.
Oh, yes there is.
Whatcha doin', Suzie?
We can't just let him keep attacking us.
Here, kitty-kitty...
There you are.
Impressive.

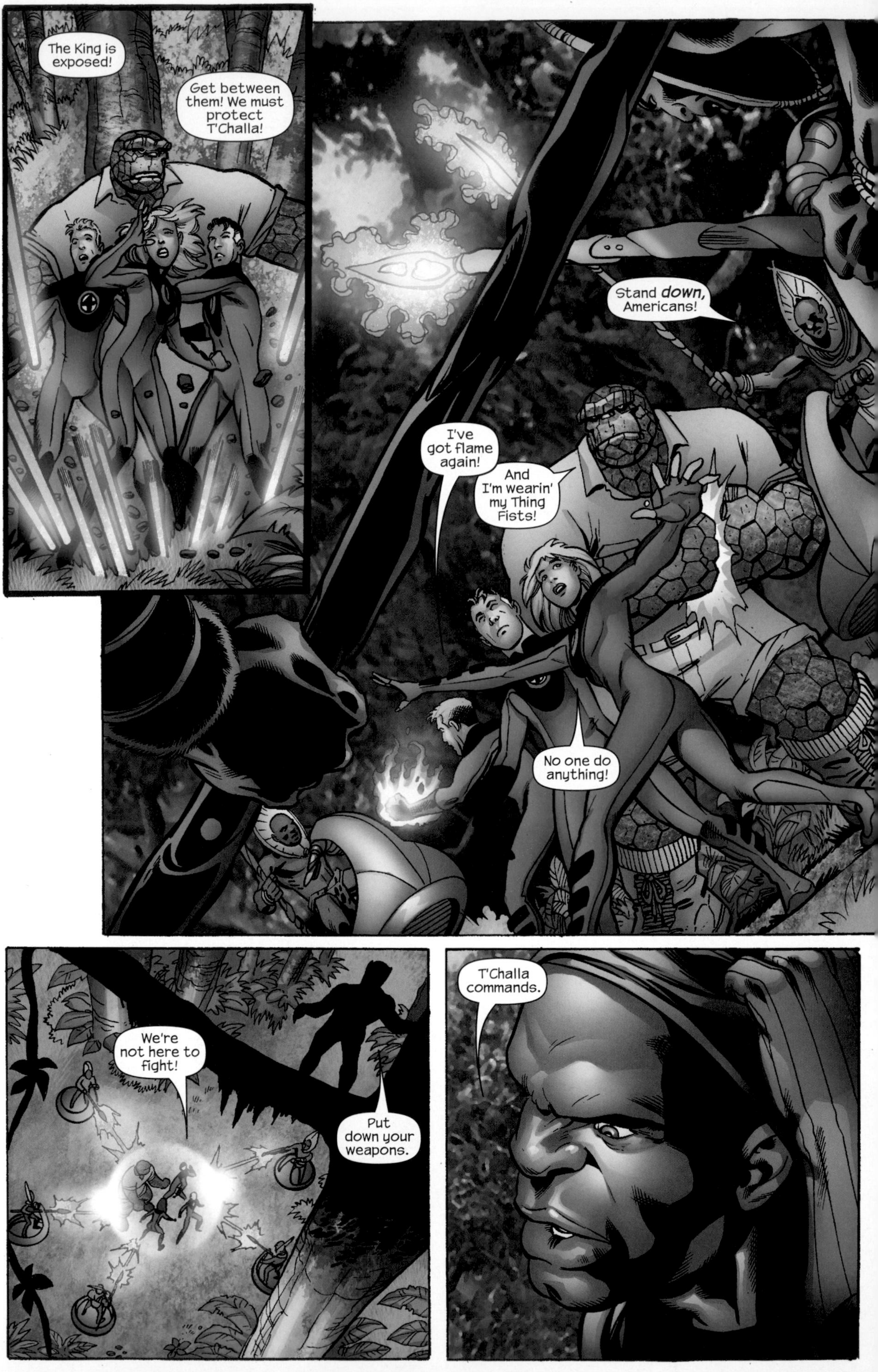
The King is exposed!
Get between them! We must protect T'Challa!
Stand *down,* Americans!
I've got flame again!
And I'm wearin' my Thing Fists!
No one do anything!
We're not here to fight!
Put down your weapons.
T'Challa commands.

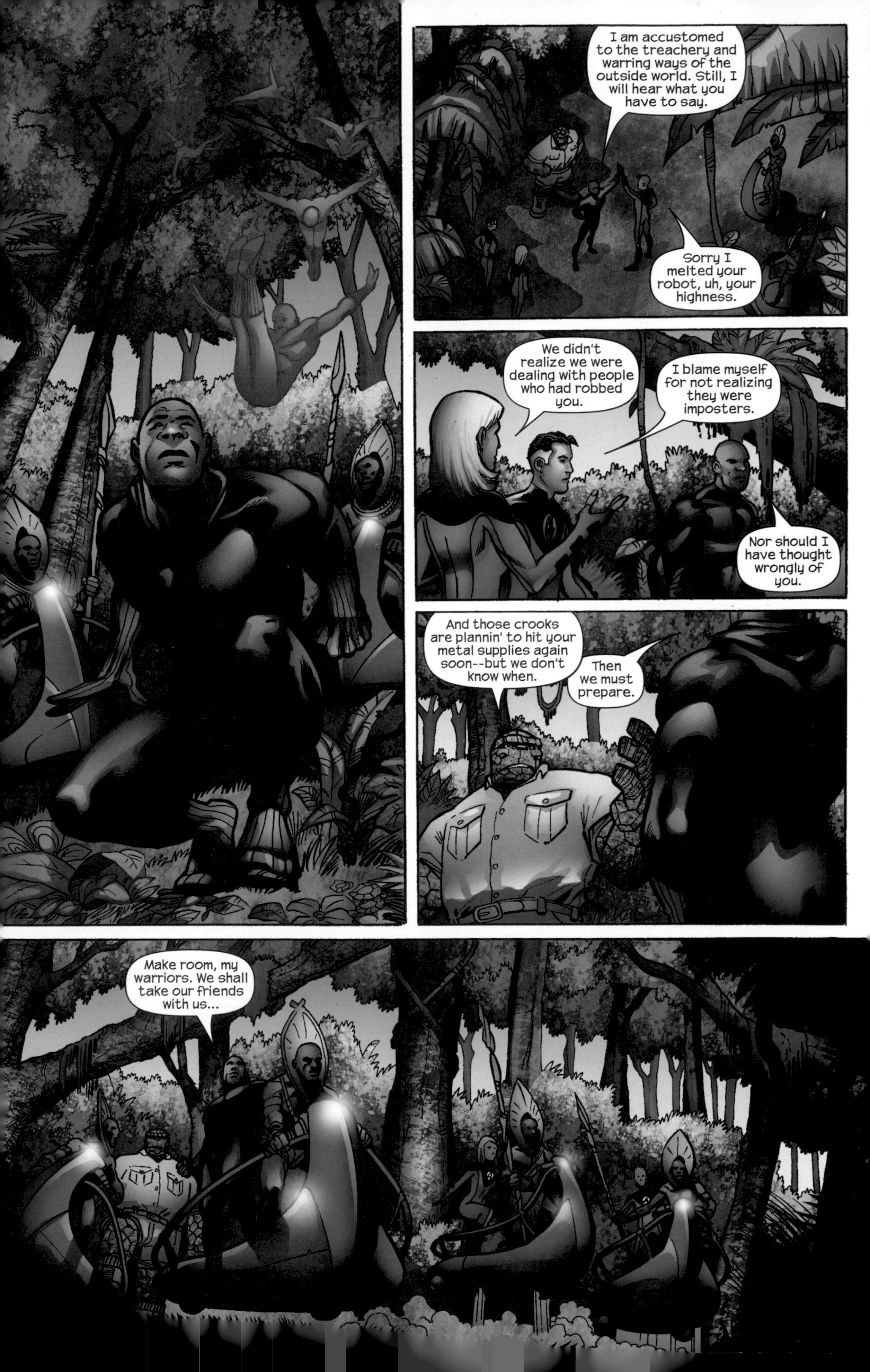
I am accustomed to the treachery and warring ways of the outside world. Still, I will hear what you have to say.
Sorry I melted your robot, uh, your highness.
We didn't realize we were dealing with people who had robbed you.
I blame myself for not realizing they were imposters.
Nor should I have thought wrongly of you.
And those crooks are plannin' to hit your metal supplies again soon--but we don't know when.
Then we must prepare.
Make room, my warriors. We shall take our friends with us...

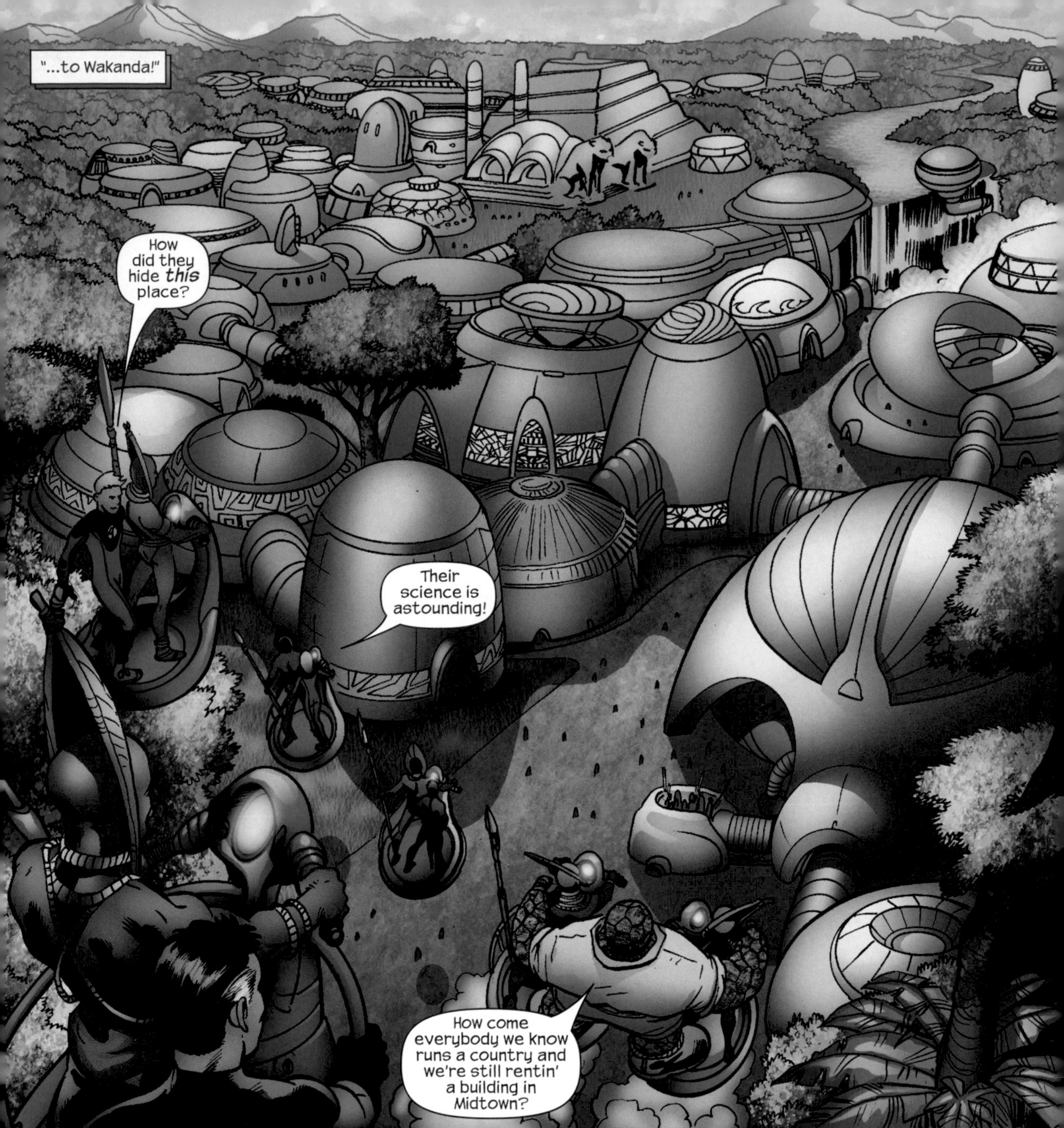
"...to Wakanda!"
How did they hide *this* place?
Their science is astounding!
How come everybody we know runs a country and we're still rentin' a building in Midtown?

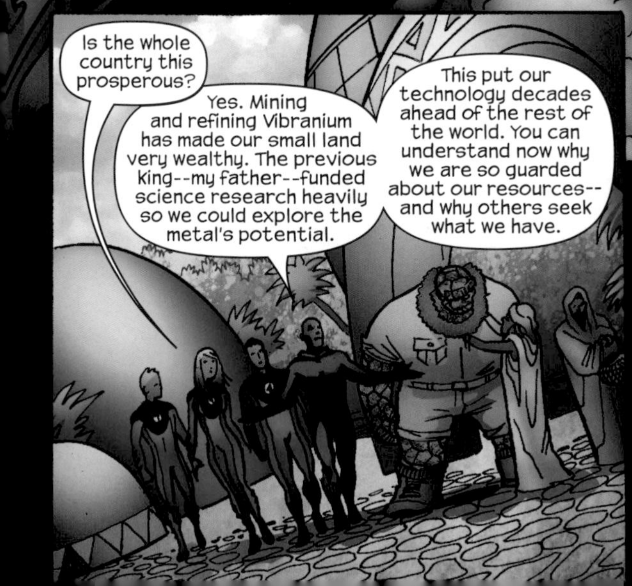
Is the whole country this prosperous?
Yes. Mining and refining Vibranium has made our small land very wealthy. The previous king--my father--funded science research heavily so we could explore the metal's potential.
This put our technology decades ahead of the rest of the world. You can understand now why we are so guarded about our resources--and why others seek what we have.

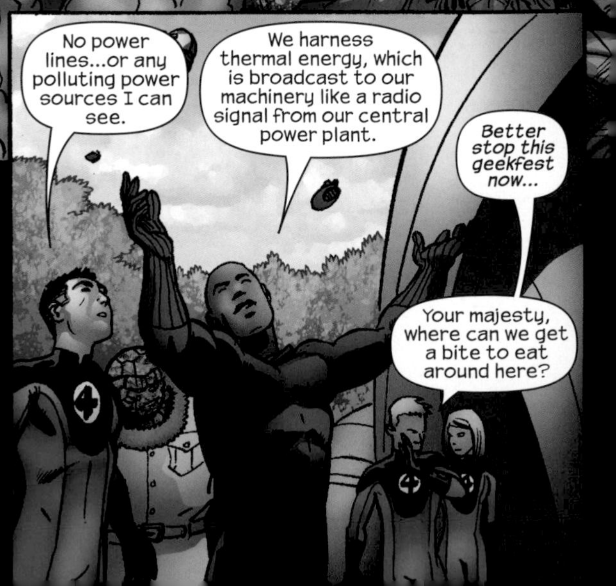
No power lines...or any polluting power sources I can see.
We harness thermal energy, which is broadcast to our machinery like a radio signal from our central power plant.
Better stop this geekfest now...
Your majesty, where can we get a bite to eat around here?

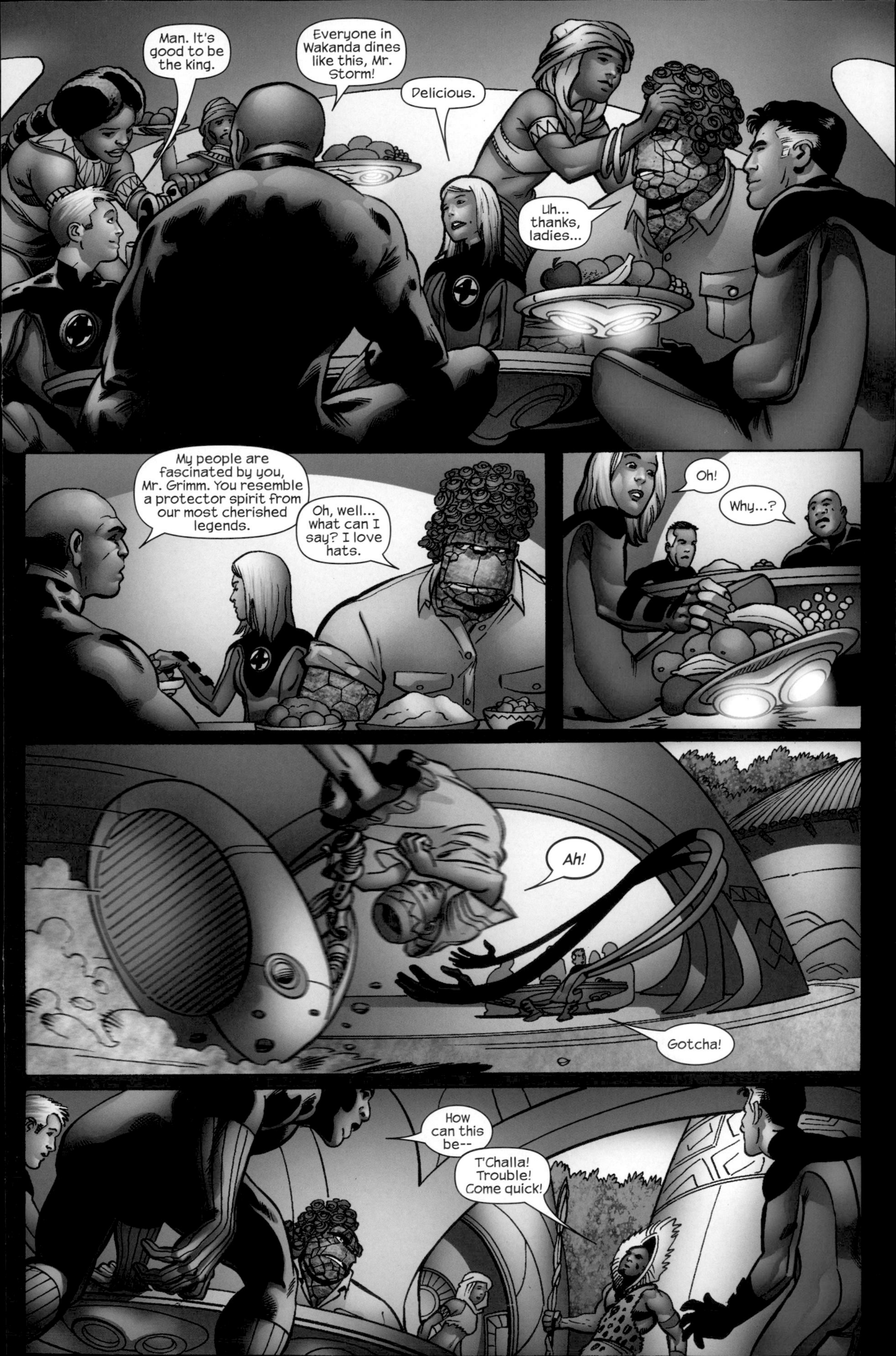
Man. It's good to be the king.
Everyone in Wakanda dines like this, Mr. Storm!
Delicious.
Uh... thanks, ladies...
My people are fascinated by you, Mr. Grimm. You resemble a protector spirit from our most cherished legends.
Oh, well... what can I say? I love hats.
Oh!
Why...?
Ah!
Gotcha!
How can this be--
T'Challa! Trouble! Come quick!

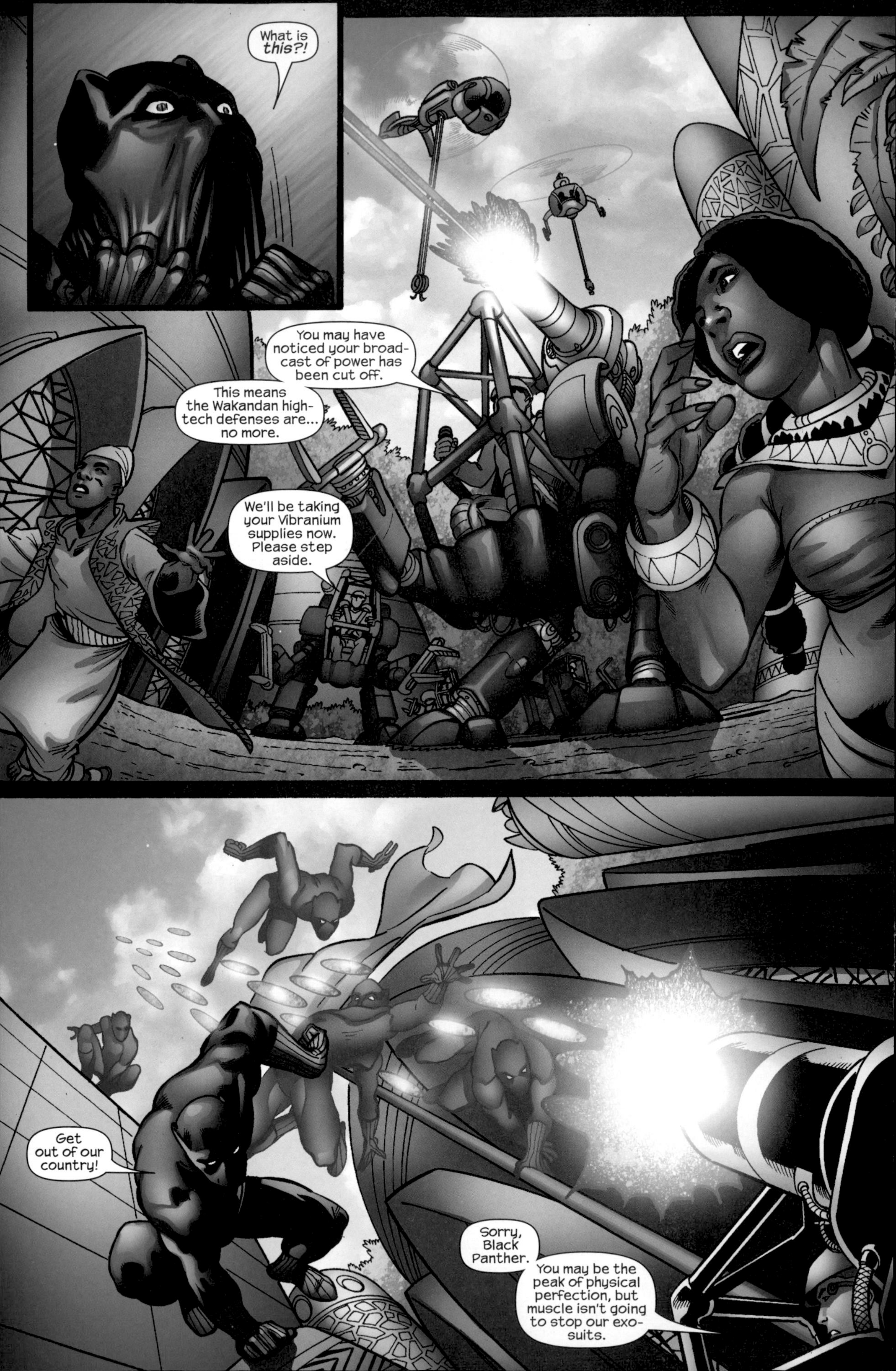

What is this?!
You may have noticed your broadcast of power has been cut off.
This means the Wakandan high-tech defenses are... no more.
We'll be taking your Vibranium supplies now. Please step aside.
Get out of our country!
Sorry, Black Panther.
You may be the peak of physical perfection, but muscle isn't going to stop our exo-suits.

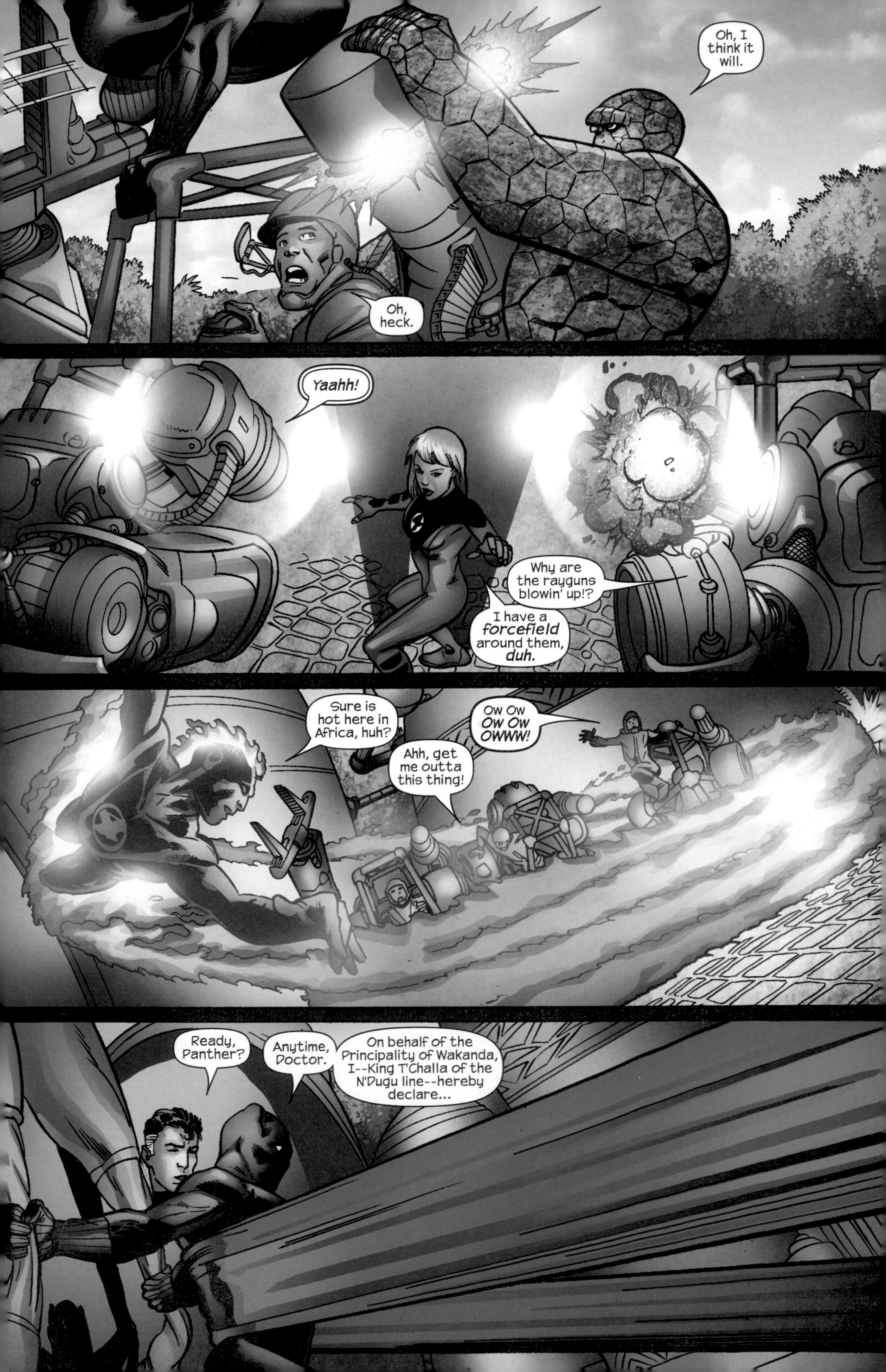
Oh, I think it will.
Oh, heck.
Yaahh!
Why are the rayguns blowin' up!?
I have a forcefield around them, duh.
Sure is hot here in Africa, huh?
Ow Ow Ow Ow OWWW!
Ahh, get me outta this thing!
Ready, Panther?
Anytime, Doctor.
On behalf of the Principality of Wakanda, I--King T'Challa of the N'Dugu line--hereby declare...

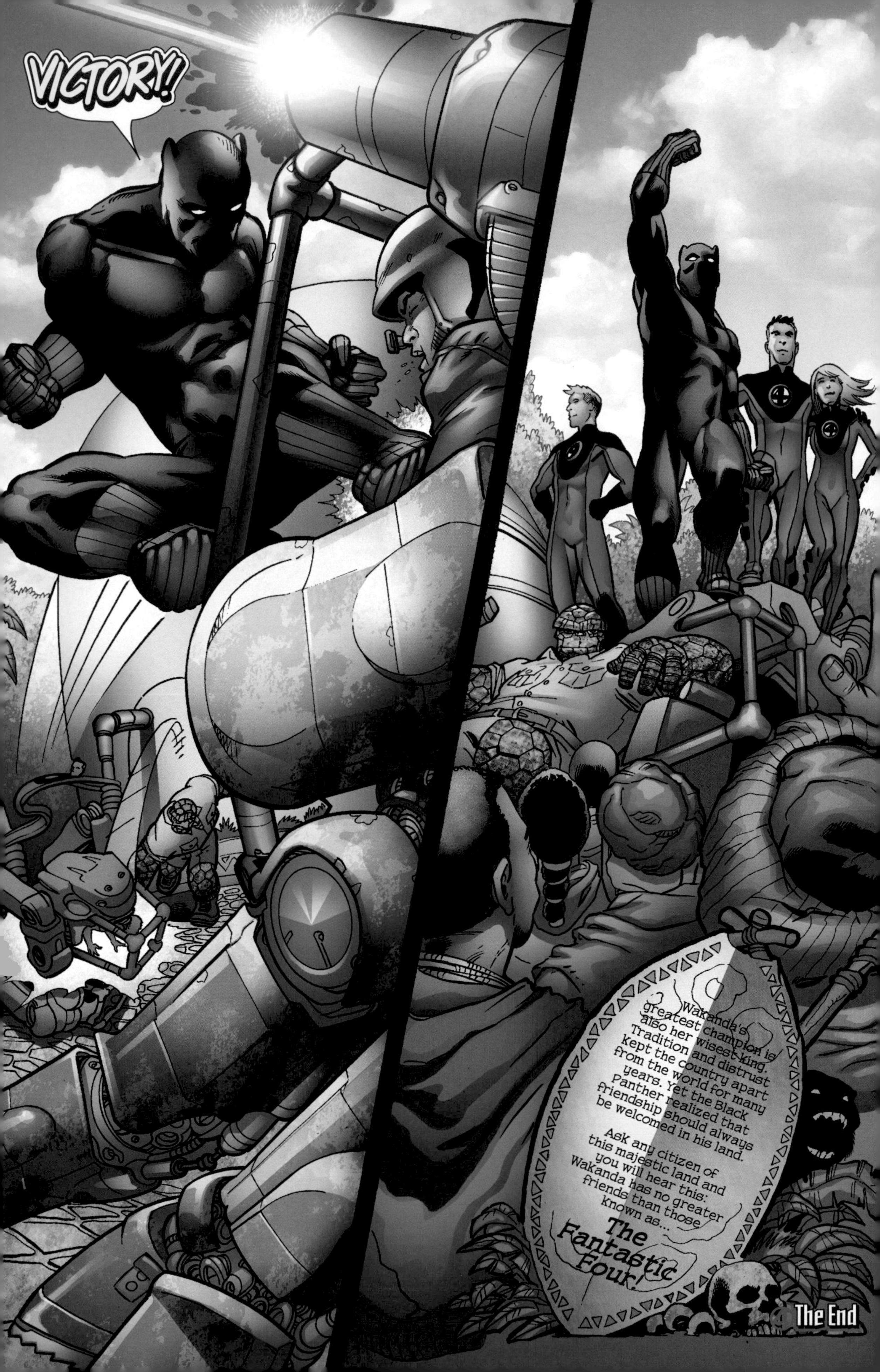
VICTORY!!
Wakanda's greatest champion is also her wisest king. Tradition and distrust kept the country apart from the world for many years. Yet the Black Panther realized that friendship should always be welcomed in his land.
Ask any citizen of this majestic land and you will hear this: Wakanda has no greater friends than those known as...
The Fantastic Four!
The End